fractured lit

To receive new fiction, contest deadlines,
and other curated content right to
your inbox, send an email to
newsletter@fracturedlit.com

Fractured Lit Volume I
Stories Selected by Kathy Fish
Edited by Tommy Dean

Front cover design by Chelsea Wales
Interior design by Cynthia Young

First printing.

ISBN: 978-1-7363695-3-1
Printed in the USA

fractured lit

VOLUME I

contents

introduction

Every Fourth of July my parents gave us kids our own packs of sparklers. My dad would instruct us to hold them out at arm's length while he set them alight. There was always that moment of anticipation as we waited for our sparklers to spit and crackle to sulfurous life. Sometimes all we could do is stare, mesmerized by their light, or we'd run around the yard with them held high above our heads, trailing fire. We loved to loop them in neon cursive, then watch as our names floated magically a beat or two longer in the night air.

Good flash fiction has the same brief, bright, sparkling intensity; the same tendency to linger. By its brevity, flash fiction announces its urgency on the page, as if to say: This story must be told right now and quickly. Its urgency resonates like an afterimage.

I am so honored to introduce the brilliant flash fiction collected in these pages.

Many thanks to Editor-in-Chief Tommy Dean for inviting me to select the final stories for inclusion in this, *Fracture Lit's* debut anthology. It was no easy task. All of the stories I was given were in some way moving or unique or dazzling. I am told the standard of stories submitted in general was extremely high. I wish all could have been included.

What a pleasure for me to encounter lines like this:

"There were aliens in What Cheer, Iowa…

And this:

> *"What are they doing? Nobody knows, your father will
> say. Close your peepers. Everything will be over soon."*

And, oh, the sheer delight of this:

> *"They met in Dayton in 1952 and fell in love in one
> minute-forty-nine seconds. . . "*

What never fails to win my heart are fresh uses of language; surprising, yet inevitable landings; the guts to explore complex emotional terrain; and all things fearlessly weird. You'll find these in abundance here.

I hope you are as captivated by these stories as much as I was. I hope you come away from this collection secure in the knowledge that the state of flash fiction today is strong. That now more than ever, flash is its own powerful and unique literary form, alive and electric and lasting.

—Kathy Fish

1

Account For What You Have

ALEXANDRA BLOGIER

First, blanch the peaches. Run them under cold water to peel their skin away. Feel the flesh underneath. This is the last thing your mother taught you—get your house in order. The heat is urgent and unforgiving, but soon you will be far from here.

The storm will hit the coasts, both east and west. The house you are in is on a cliff on a curve of ocean. It will not last the night. The house you are going to is small and without windows, for there is nothing there to see. It won't take long to get to the property, acres of land so flat they make you feel desperate and unmoored like you could wander into the grass one day and never be found.

Buying the land was Hannah's idea.

Maybe one day we'll look back on these as the dark days of our early adulthood, she had written to you in a letter when she was traveling aimlessly around the country, winding her way around and down. You were twenty years old and could feel someone else's heartbeat pump through your body. You didn't mean to get pregnant, didn't mean to stay pregnant, but you had already stopped making active decisions, already started letting things happen to you. You were a motherless daughter with an avocado inside you, blooming into a daughter of your own. You knew, by then, that those were the last days you had.

When Hannah called to tell you about the land she found in the middle of the country, you knew you would say yes. She was the first person you had spoken to in weeks and her voice over the phone was far away, but she spoke evenly and clearly and you thought of that exhibit you and she had gone to as children, the one where you stuck your hand into a box and felt something spiky or squishy, something completely foreign to your closed eyes and reaching fingers, only to open the box and find it was something familiar, something you had known all along.

Holy fuck, she said, when she saw you. She laughed a wild laugh and buried you in her arms and did not let go, and you knew then that you were bringing your baby into a world you could manage.

You spent the next two weeks sleeping in a tent, carrying water from a well in buckets, watching Hannah haul wood and build your home.

I can help, you told her. I'm not that pregnant.

Any pregnant is that pregnant, she said.

How did you learn to build a house?

How did you learn to make a baby?

She lay down next to you, head to your head, and you braided your hair into one long strand.

What if I can't do this? You asked. It was the first time you voiced that fear. You can, she said.

You will. She did not look at you. You don't really have a choice.

And then she was born, your avocado that swelled into a melon and pushed out into the world as a tiny wailing creature, and you knew just what to do. Nurse her when she was hungry, listen to her lungs pull in air. These things were no longer hard. They were choices you no longer needed to make.

You wake up one morning and the spiders have spread their tangled webs across the earth. Their silken husks cover every branch of forest, as though they built their homes as they were fleeing. This is how you know the storm is here. It is a tectonic shift; it is bigger than you thought it would be. It will do more than flood the coasts, it will split the Earth apart and fill it back up with water. Your knees buckle and you are on the floor, thinking, Oh, I didn't know bodies could do that. You are gasping for air, you are choking on nothing, and then you hear the baby cry out in her crib. The only thing you can do is go to her, kiss her along her fragile spine, and say, listen to your body, listen to what it is telling you. You did not expect the world you shared with her to be like this.

You drive for hours, the baby asleep in the back. The mason jars clink with every turn you make, chimes that tell you there will be enough food for a few weeks, nothing more. The rain has started in sheets, the phones have already stopped working and you know Hannah will be waiting for you, her shadowy outline in the doorway. We can do this, you hear her saying to you, we can make this work. There is a dull buzz in your brain as you get closer to the Property, a frequency you cannot ignore.

Steam rises on the road that is filled not with cars but with people, spilling across both lanes. You wonder if they know something you do not, if maybe you should not be in your car but among the swarm. You turn to face the baby. She is staring at you and you say, baby, I'm here. Darling, I'm right here. In months, these people will be nothing but bones pacing the empty earth. The houses you pass will decay down to their lonely frames. How many times can you truly start over? There is one turn left to make, but you don't stop, you don't even consider stopping. You do not say goodbye to Hannah, if only because you don't know how.

Keep going into the darkness. Head towards the coast, already crumbling. Do not slow down, do not look behind you to the land fading fast. Do not calm the baby as she is crying. Do not lift your foot until you are over the canyon. Close your eyes and do not look down.

⁓

ALEXANDRA BLOGIER is a writer living in Boston, Massachusetts and along the edge of Cape Cod. She is the author of the *YA* novel *The Last Girl on Earth*.

2

As Solid As an Ashtray and Emits More Smoke

EDIE MEADE

It is a cast-iron frying pan filled with cigarette butts. The handle is just the right size for my hand and just out of reach on the freezer. It is an ashtray. That's all it is, and I don't want it.

"You don't want that," Momma has told me many times, so I try not to. Momma is smoking a cigarette and quartering chickens on the top of the deep freezer, where the bloody water runs down yellow, yolkish. She moves the frying pan closer to her when I come near but does not wipe the trickle. I pat the freezer, so cold inside but so warm along this wall, and the chicken-water wets me. It is a tight spot at the back of the house where the kitchen meets the back bedroom, where Daddy keeps the fire burning with morsels of tractor tire.

I stand in the bedroom doorway and look in at Daddy, who smiles as if he has just come back from far away. I smile back without anything to say. A brown blanket over the window keeps the room amber-dark all day long, but I'm not allowed in there except to say good night. It's not time to say good night, so I watch Daddy polish his boots from the threshold. He sits on the edge of the bed, legs crossed like a woman. One leg has a lot of muscle but the other one is thin because he stepped on a grenade in Vietnam. He crosses the thin leg over the top and he can't feel whether it's uncomfortable or not. The thin leg doesn't fall asleep. It prickles all on its own, he says.

On the footboard of the bed, a cut-crystal jewel collects ashes. It's an ashtray, too. Daddy's cigarette is burning into a rope of ash all by itself.

"Come on out of there," Momma says, slopping something into the scrap bucket. Her arms have the same goosebumps as the chicken skin. I edge back on the threshold and pull a wet pinfeather from the ruching of my blouse. The facets of the crystal ashtray turn the blanket-curtain light lavender, yellow. If I had my way I would stand at the footboard, the warmth of the fire on my back, and look through the glass at Daddy. But this is as close as I can go until it's time to say good night.

I don't know why Daddy polishes his boots, but he does it every day. His boots are massive, black, with a hundred eyelets and a mile of laces. Their stiffness helps him walk even if he can't feel much in his leg. On the sole of his thin-leg boot, he tacked on a wedge of old tractor tire, to make his legs the same length. It helps even out his limp. Daddy polishes his boots with boar-bristle brushes that he keeps in a wooden shoeshine box. His box is full of shoe polish tins, round ones with crimped lids I can open with my teeth.

I cannot open the tin of Momma's sewing supplies, having chipped my tooth trying. Tins are hard to open for a reason. Daddy hands the polish to me and lets me try. He smiles as my mouth puckers. Then my chicken-water hands slick up the lid and his face darkens.

Vietnam is a place, and also a war before I was born. It is located just past the bedroom doorframe. It is as solid an object as an ashtray and emits more smoke. I don't want it, so I try to leave it alone, forget about it.

Like many things, shoe polish is bitter and leaves a lasting residue.

"Don't put that in your mouth," Momma tells me. She pinches her words around the cigarette on her lip and I notice she has moved the frying pan again. In another house, perhaps one that existed before and further away from Vietnam, it would be a child's toy, perfectly sized for cooking pretend eggs. But in this house, it is an ashtray.

I wipe the tin on my blouse until the kiwi on the top is bright. The black crescent in my ruching won't come out, though Momma will try. I return the polish to Daddy's palm and calm returns to the facets of his face.

～

EDIE MEADE is a writer, visual artist, and mother of four boys in Huntington, West Virginia. She is passionate about literacy and collects books like they're going out of style. Say hi on Twitter @ediemeade or https://ediemeade.com/.

3

(don't)
remember me like this

CYN NOONEY

1. During the space race days your parents sip Maxwell House in the morning, Beefeater before dark. Through bedroom walls you hear talk of traveling to the moon, Viet Cong soldiers, and Brezhnev. How it's another Bay of Pigs and screw that. Over Sloppy Joe casserole ask, What's a Commie? Stick your tongue out when your brother flips you the bird. When no

one answers, wonder aloud where the pigs are, may you pet them? Walk the dog, your mother will answer

2. On the way to Dunkin Donuts after church, notice all the beat-up Chevys and Impalas plastered with bumper stickers that say *Bring Home Our POWs*. Observe the drivers' twitchy fingers, pinched lips. Ask your father what POW means. Pronounce the letters like a pistol's report—*pow pow pow*. Not like an acronym. You don't know what one of those is but you do know about guns. Right then your brother will jam a fake one into your ribs—point an index finger at his crotch. If your father pretends not to hear, ask again. Louder. Just a little bit. With the exhale of his Winston filter learn POW means unlucky. Like you, your brother will hiss. Now roll over. Play dead.

3. Down the street from your house is an army base called Fort Carson. You've always liked the sound of that. Anything with *fort* in it sounds fun. Your brother and his friend build one in the backyard, scrawl on the door *No Girls Allowed*. For Halloween let your mother dress you up as a flower child, smear gaudy rouge across your cheeks, press a faded pillow-case into your palm. Hoist the cardboard sign she painted, *Make Love, Not War*, when you step onto porches and ring the bell. Some of the women who answer the door will shriek before slamming it in your face. Ask your mother why they didn't give you candy. She will sigh, It's all rotten anyway.

4. At the midnight drive-in where your parents believe you'll conk out while they watch *Goodbye Columbus* and *Easy Rider*—prove them wrong. Peer spellbound in your flannel pink pajamas from the jump seat of a VW Bug until you can't contain yourself any longer and ask in a squirrely voice, What are they doing? Nobody knows, your father will say. Close your peepers. Everything will be over soon. When your

brother pops up, slug him hard. He will smirk, Some day you'll do the nasty too.

5. Each month when the magazine arrives wrapped in brown paper, note how quickly your father snags it from the pile of mail and hoofs it downstairs to the tiny half-bathroom. See your mother fill a wine glass to the brim, carry it to the couch, mumble in the dark, *Nothingbutamansworld*. Yell after your father, Why can't you read that up here? Let me be, he will call over his shoulder. Give a man peace.

6. One Saturday when you can't fall asleep, tiptoe into your brother's bedroom, nudge him awake and ask what will happen if you don't want to go to the moon. Admit you have no interest in living on cheese and floating around weightlessly. I've never been good at floating, you say. What will happen if I don't want to go? He'll roll over and belch Rocky Mountain Coors piss-breath. Simple, he will mutter as he wipes crust from your eyes, you will end up all alone.

7. Toward the end of ninth grade find your mother spread-eagled on the couch, eyelids fluttering, the balding neighbor from across the street rummaging beneath her skirt. Like a pig rooting for truffles, you tell your brother—they didn't even hear me come in. How can I ever look at her the same? Let it slide, you brother will urge. She's probably trying to feel something. Or get even.

8. After college graduation visit your brother in a windswept apartment facing the sea. Clasp his shadowy hand, whisper, I'm here, ask, What can I do? He is gossamer thin, sports blotches the size of cigar burns. As he puffs each word of, Please don't remember me like this, your parents—no longer married—can be heard arguing on the stairs. Bring a blanket to his chin, tease, You're leaving me with *them*? Step toward

the door to let them in, stop when he commands, Not yet —first you must promise. Pledge with your whole sloppy heart then say, But I'll be mad at you forever. Flip him the bird. Watch his papery lips crack into a grin. Hey, you will hear him whisper—forever sounds good.

CYN NOONEY received first prize in nonfiction for her piece "Here is How" in the 2020 *Chestnut Review*'s Stubborn Writers Contest. She's also published in the *New York Times*, *San Francisco Chronicle*, *805 Living*, and other publications. She is currently working on her memoir.

4

Evening Clay

JOSH WAGNER

The speaker made us choose:

"Your house is on fire. Family and pets are safe. What one thing would you take with you?" He hunted us with his eyes. Shoes squeaked over the gym floor, echoing in the frost of our hypnotic teenage lethargy, ". . . just *one* thing . . ."

The bell rang, and we exploded like buckshot.

That summer, wildfires funneled through the canyons toward our little five-acre plot of fenceposts and sagebrush. The bald ridge flaunted sparse pine. If the fire hit all this scrub, there'd be no stopping it.

What would I take?

Dad built the house for my mother before I was born. Last year she took her own life in the gully where, in autumn, elk descend by the hundreds. We'd constructed a memorial with a cedar bench, iron cross, and a ring of standing stones.

Everything I valued now was part of the earth. Flames might blacken the stones, singe the cross, ash the bench. Scorch the ground where she offered parting words to a starlit sky. Sometimes I'd go down and listen for their echo.

"We'll have to move," Dad said.

"They'll put it out. They always do."

The evacuation order gave us 48-hours.

SUNSET BROUGHT TRACES of smoke over the hills. We spent the day hauling boxes to our new apartment. I grabbed two beers for one last walk down to the cross and stones. I sat on the bench, watching silver sage turn purple. I imagined the ridge going up like a phoenix glaze of cloud-feathers molding renegade light into evening clay.

Most of my anger had fizzled out. Only cold heat remained, trapped in brittle stone. I'd stopped asking why she didn't stick around to see me graduate, write a book, start a family… Now I ask why our world still can't soothe agony raw enough to blot out such dreams.

What would she have taken with her, given the chance, in flight from the burning house of her mind? Leaving me crippled, a coal in the grass, desperate for an evening gust. My whole life ahead of me, which really isn't any time at all.

Only sparks now. I had to choose.

I emptied her beer at the base of the cross. A fresh glow licked the horizon.

If you could take just one thing...

Then I heard her voice. Like an echo under all that ash.

Take the fire.

⌒⌒

JOSH WAGNER is a novelist and playwright from Missoula, Montana, with a Creative Writing MSc from the University of Edinburgh. His work has been described as lyric, whimsical, and incisive. He is the author of four novels and three graphic novels, and has won awards for his work in comics and theatre. His short stories and poetry have been published by *Cafe Irreal, Not One of Us* (Clarity), *Medulla Review, Lovecraft eZine, Cleaver Magazine, Asymmetrical Press*, and *Image Comics*. He enjoys rhizomes, paradoxes, and thinks left unsaid.

5

Girl in the Snow

WENDY OLESON

He'd be back soon, and she was glad to be cold. From the passenger's seat, she'd watched him float up the dark path. His footsteps remained, half-inch depressions in new snow. It fell—blue-tinted gobs of it, the kind that made children's mouths water—sticky snowflakes that tilted chins skyward and opened mouths wide.

She had decided to wait. She had asked him to turn off the engine. It wasn't that cold, and they didn't need to be wasteful. He'd taken his keys. It'd be quick, he'd said, like ripping off a bandage, and he'd return to her with snow in his hair and on his shoulders. She'd brush it off, make him tingle at her touch.

His figure disappeared into the cluster of apartments; it had been necessary to park the car that far away. She couldn't have gone in with him, even if she'd wanted. Even if she was desperately curious. Her presence would be salt in the wound. She understood. She understood him—that's why he'd chosen her. She wasn't worried. If she was worried at all, it was about that shared dog, that his love for the yappy thing would make him lose his nerve. Dumb dog.

The car smelled minty—maybe it was her breath—and it felt warm enough. Not comfortable, but warm enough with her mittens and scarf. Other cars lined the road. Not many. She counted three, four, but the bend made it hard to be sure. The cars weren't cars anymore, their backs rounded with heaps of dirty snow. Old snow caked in ice. She felt sorry for their owners. Useless cars frozen in place. How many times had the snow plow ruched up another wall of it? Only a persistent sun could free the metal beasts.

Those cars weren't her problem though. She couldn't see through the windshield any longer, and she couldn't bring herself to get out of the car to clear it. She'd lose too much heat. The snow would come back. A Sisyphean task. Winter was worthless.

There were always summer stories of idiots leaving dogs and babies in hot cars, but you didn't hear much about freezing. Cold was slow, the Earth warming. Each year there'd be more news about the infirm perishing, bodies slumped in rocking chairs, window fans shorted out. The stink they'd leave! She was glad to be cold and wiggled her fingers inside the mittens. She'd knitted him a pair in olive green because she believed he would do it—was surely doing it this very moment!—and he'd be quick, back any second, relieved to be done. He was doing it for them. Then, they could get their own dog (despite her allergies), a big one. A better one. An explosion of white fur! A dog to pull their baby's wagon. Was she blushing? Such warmth in her cheeks. She couldn't see through the windows, but he was coming. This was love, that thing she'd been waiting for, and he had to come now. So much snow falling, her spine bore the roof's bow. The anticipation was a sweetness, a pleasure, because what a sight it would be, what a blessing, when he scraped away the snow and opened the door to her—waves of snow, a Hallelujah, the black sky white with snow—him lunging toward her, all reward for her patience—her faith without fear—and she'd kiss him madly, his one and only, her mouth opening and opening: her body warm pooling honey where he'd beg to swim.

WENDY OLESON's flash fiction has appeared most recently in *Atticus Review, Denver Quarterly, The Adroit Journal,* and *Fourteen Hills.* She is the author of two award-winning prose chapbooks (from *Gertrude Press* and *Map Literary*) and serves as managing editor for *Split Lip Magazine.* She lives with her wife and dogs in Walla Walla, Washington.

6

Girl on a Bike,
Boy in Dayton

JOHN BENSINK

Jack is sixteen when he sees Marie the first time, then eighty-four when he sees her again, though he doesn't know he saw her before, and those caring for him—tolerating him—wouldn't believe him anyway, for the brain is falling away from the man, who's always looking blank-inward and couldn't be seeing much of anything at this point, and clinically sees less every day. But he's got this crack of a smile lately, thin but it never goes away, as if some long-awaited wish has been delivered and, now that it's finally here, it can never be taken away.

So weak, this old Marie, and trouble breathing, never without her oxygen tubing, a wispy frail that most avoid looking at too long not because she's not knocking on Death's Door, she's *pounding* on it—so close to stepping through, people might fear she'd pull them in with her if they're too close. But Marie, terrified on her arrival, has calmed; where there was quaking, there is now a gracious serenity. She seems fearless now and … if staff were surprised to see her *alive* yet one more day, imagine how amazed they are at an insouciant old lady who, despite shuffling to her wheelchair, can't wait to get out of her room and get to breakfast and then whatever the next thing might be. *Carefree*, at her age, laughing, even with that old failing heart coming apart like a cheap engine that was never assembled properly to start with.

THEY MET IN Dayton in 1952 and fell in love in one minute-forty-nine seconds—the duration of their time together. It was a summer trip with his father, checking in on hardware accounts, bring the boy along from Lancaster, let him see some of the world and what his old man did in it.

Girl on a bike, blue fenders, wicker basket leading the handlebars. Green-and-yellow checked dress, blonde braids draping down her back, saddle shoes a lot like his. She kickstanded it carefully out front, Jack watching her from inside as his father showed the owner a new hinge line he repped.

Marie entered and the bell jingled and Jack looked away fast so he could pretend he just happened to look up at the sound but she was onto him even though she was only fourteen—onto him before she realized she was onto him, somehow. There was a *snap* across the space between them, a cable connecting them and getting tauter as she crossed to the counter and their hearts pounded the same roar.

The owner pushed two quarts and a pint of paint he had mixed forward, then asked if the boy could help the girl load them up. Jack waited for nothing, grabbing the two quarts as she reached in for the pint and body-voltage surged back and forth as his hand grazed hers, then a *look*, stop-time like in the movies, and he was walking her out front, the two adults going back to their hinges.

After the jolt came bottomless shyness. Whatever this was ... it couldn't be anything, could it –kids, what do they know? The cautious walk side by side, avoiding eyes, then placing the paint in her basket—another hand-graze as crackly as before. Kids, they know nothing, but somehow, they know this is everything. A minute where nothing is said (nothing is ever said, really), then she smiles and nods thanks and mounts her bike and pedals off. Sixty feet away she looks back over her shoulder and there's Jack, staring, smiling, and she pedals away fast, braids whipping and bouncing on her back in the splashy sun and though they can't remember it now, they also never forgot it.

THE HEART IS always at work—monitoring itself for problems and creating solutions. It fixes itself endlessly, a squad of brain, blood, and electricity always working and finding ways to stretch out the beats and outplay the inevitable failure. Marie's heart started pulling apart when she was eight, but no one knew, it was such a small disintegration—slow, at the cellular level.

She thought he must have moved to Dayton and she would surely see him again. She thought she would go around a corner and there's that big square face with the apologetic eyes and the farm-boy smile. She thought about him for a long time, but then she stopped thinking about him ... but a part of her that she forgot about never stopped thinking about him.

The heart is a genius, but the brain is a hundred hearts—a thousand. So many sectors of Jack's brain are closed off, nonregenerative, some behind rusted-shut doors that will likely never open again, others down tunnels that have been dynamited and for practical purposes never existed—uncountable collapses that sucked away whole decades of his life, people, places, and emotions included.

But the Ohio girl: the area that holds her is as alive as the day it formed in him—even stronger. Jack forgot about her but *it* didn't—it's independent of him and now, so sturdy and resurgent, when so much of him is gone, it signaled to her; and it signaled, *through her*, all the people who decide for her. So last week they brought her to this assisted living complex in Pennsylvania, back-dropped by the Allegheny National Forest, with a south-facing patio looking onto quilty fields and a lead-gray river.

It signaled to staff to put them, the best-behaved residents in the complex, side by side on the patio, she with the failing but deter-mined heart, he with the addled brain but for the one perfect part.

Marie is too weak to speak; the place he speaks from is dead. But outside in their wheelchairs, faint sun just warm enough, there is no need. They don't know each other but they know each other completely. They do not speak, they have never spoken a word, but they have also never stopped speaking, across all these years.

JOHN BENSINK's recent short fiction publications include *Glimmer Train* and *Hollywood Dementia.com*. He lives in Pittsburgh in a small town on the Ohio River, and is busily at work on a collection of short stories set in this region.

7

Grandma Kim at Forty-Five: A Serigraph in Four Layers

CHLOE CHUN SEIM

1/10

Grandma Kim had a rose-petal mouth. See the ballooned lips, half-inch creases trapping her mouth at each end. Such shapes are difficult to translate in their three-dimensional splendor on paper. She smiles, but a printed smile is not a living smile. I would like to have seen her grin for myself, but then again, art is the playground for reanimating the dead.

2/10

Grandma Kim curled her hair, her pretty black hair, our mother says, showing us the formless crimps of her own broken and burned hair. What a mistake. Our grandma's hair could be like ivy when left to its good nature: voracious. Here she has pinned it down, her bangs the only moving part and they, too, show little of her unmuted self.

3/10

This print is of my grandmother, whom I never knew, and so it is of my mother and my sister and myself, too. You cannot see her large front teeth or the slight bowing of her calves or the delicate arc of her nose, but I tell you they are there, and in my mother and my sister and me, too. Her body divided into my mother divided into my sister and me.

4/10

Screen printing demands that you separate the world into discrete layers, but so too does it force you to see the glory made in over-lapping them. Blue ink overlays gold and soars into a fertile green so that my grandmother's garden pops, as it must have then, so much care given to the nurturing of things. See that birth. Note the flush of her tomato vines. Observe the hard lines that separate my grandmother's hair, her body, from the background. No such lines exist in this world.

5/10

Each layer: run a test, note the placement with tape, pull fast and with strength and without breathing. Too slow, this layer, the gold of my grandma's skin, which also blends with the plush blue of my grandma's sky to create the green foliage. The paper has stuck to the screen and now my grandma's unblemished skin and her garden are pocked and bubbled, the ink left reaching toward you. This, too, is natural.

6/10

Places can be haunted, we are told, but people must be haunted, too. If ghosts are souls turned vaporous and their homes confined spaces, then surely they can occupy a body? My mother always spoke of hauntings in her adulthood, before I or my sister came. Of a crushing feeling over her legs as she slept. Of sounds and voices that had no physical birth. She always believed her apartments to be haunted. She never considered that it was her bones, her blood that sabotaged her. Her hauntings stopped only because my grandmother channeled herself into me before birth. See the doubling of the linework, impossible without running the ink twice, and I tell you, you see, in those twinned grandmothers, her ghost making herself known. She deserves to be known.

7/10

Grandma Kim wore an apron even when she walked my mother and her sisters to school. Even when she went to the movies. The only time she ever untied its strings, our mother says, is when she would go to church with my mother and her sisters or when she would lay with her husband, who neither attended church nor went to the movies, so that he only ever saw her hips free when they made love. Note the fraying here, the delicate wash from a clean cream to the gritty brown marking years of use. We call this a rainbow pull, the melding of two colors in one layer. Some rainbows are not vibrant. Some rainbows are dishwater.

8/10

See the fumbling of the sky, the ink that just kissed the surface of the paper, leaving so much desire in its wake. My mother says that our grandmother was a perfectionist, every garment sewn in rigid lines. No errant threads. You might call me a bad grandson for presenting the unruly and off-kilter versions of this print, but let me remind you that to honor your ancestors you must build on their triumphs. A seamless garment. A seams-bared serigraph.

9/10

You might say this was not the assignment. You might say that you asked for ten matching prints, and I tell you that these are the same. Identical in their sloppiness, their mishaps. No more perfect symmetry exists than in the misguided, the malformed, the tainted.

10/10

Grandma Kim was born in Seoul and died in Kansas, not even seventy, not even a grandmother yet. Riddled, my mother says. She was riddled with tumors. A hard life takes its toll in hidden ways and yet, my grandmother kept going, even in death, to know my mother, to know me. She spent her years escaping to Tokyo, escaping to my grandfather's barracks, escaping to his American home with its American layers, so opaque, so unreadable. See her spirit in these eyes. See her reading you and everyone else, finally, with the clarity of the unbounded. With the eyes of the immortal.

〜

CHLOE CHUN SEIM is a writer living in Lawrence, Kansas. Her work has appeared or is forthcoming in *North American Review, Yemassee, Hobart, Potomac Review, McNeese Review,* and others. She won the 2021 Anton Chekov Award for Flash Fiction from *Litmag,* and her short story collection was recently selected as a finalist for the *St. Lawrence Book Award.* She holds an MFA from the University of Missouri, Kansas City.

8

i chose the pencil

RICHARD SCHWARZENBERGER

The receptionist, who I thought might be a robot, told me I could fill out the form online or else in the office with a No. 2 pencil. I chose the pencil. The hexagonal pencil, if you think about it, has a sophistication that only a highly advanced civilization could achieve.

One of the questions on the application form was, *What is your favorite electrical device?* Tough question. I penciled in *vacuum cleaner* because I didn't want to spend too much time thinking about it. I do love my vacuum cleaner. It's a Miele, and very faithful, although I'm not one hundred per cent convinced fidelity is a virtue I should elevate so highly. Maybe it's not my favorite device. One of my ten favorites, surely.

Ten favorites. I could do *that* list in a minute. The toaster oven would be right up there. Butter melting on a steaming slice of cinnamon raisin walnut bread. Think about it. My weedwhacker also is beloved. It's electric. It does its whacking in an offhand, genteel way, unlike gas-powered devices that slash and hiss like vipers. I would also put my hair dryer near the top of that list. It shrives my moldy thoughts with dry winds. It convinces me every morning that I am worthy of love.

Thinking about the hair dryer I was compelled to remember the motor in my vacuum is making anguished noises, and there is a smell more unpleasant than usual. I gave considerable consideration to how it might look if I erased. The scut of eraser, and the faint shadowy canyons of *vacuum cleaner*. I forged ahead. I erased, marveling, but who wouldn't, at the perfect economy of the eraser. Some whiz calculated mass of eraser-head versus probable human mistakes and this is what he or she came up with. Nothing is as depressing as a pencil with a depleted eraser. Or worse, an eraser that is petrified, that not even spit will revive. This eraser was a paragon, and *vacuum cleaner* was dispatched.

I worried that I was taking too long with the form. The receptionist was giving me a vamoose vibe. I couldn't tell exactly how I knew since she was pretending to attend to some flickering on her screen, but I knew. By then I was pretty sure she was a robot but boy howdy, I had to admire the craft, especially the skin texture and tones.

Another candidate appeared for consideration. My blender. Although the last time the cap was loose, *boom*, soup on ceiling, soup dripping down counters and out of my mustache. I was lucky not to end up in the emergency room.

Scratch the blender. I will put it on the sidewalk for someone else to have their own good times with it.

My final answer, and a very satisfying one, was my Oral-B electric toothbrush. I spark it up before bedtime, and when its programmed duration ends, my gums radiate wellness. Since I started using it my nightmares have abated. Even now when I have one, I can convince myself that nightmares are just anxieties compressed into images and not fate.

I handed in the form and gave the receptionist my full Oral-B smile. When she returned the exact smile I knew she was definitely, absolutely, without a doubt, a robot. And her skin wasn't as credible as I thought. It had a rubbery sheen.

It made sense: the business of the company was robotics. Of course they would want to know the depth of one's intimacy with machines. Trying to get a job here was a wild goose chase. My decades in Human Resources will terrify them. They will say I am too non-linear. They will press their *delete* keys and then, for spite, because even robots have a petty side, *trash*. They are programming their own extinction and they don't know it.

I couldn't find my goddamn car in the parking garage. My car is not on any Favorites List. For a half hour the Orfeo on my key chain led me into the depths. If I had a do-over I might put that thingamabob in the catbird seat instead of my Oral-B, if I knew what to call it.

Why, will someone explain to me, can they develop such intelligent machines, and the elevator is always on the fritz? Good thing I have a brand new hip and could walk the stairs. I'm not against mechanization. Other body parts are ripe for upgrading: knee, eyes, teeth. I'm thrilled with my artificial heart. Without it I wouldn't be here. I wouldn't be me.

Can a robot have a concept of 'here'? I would love to have a philosophical discussion with the RMs. They might appreciate me. They might recognize that I am potentially an abundance, a natural resource. I embody the past and the future, the wine dark sea, the topless towers of Trebizond. I contain multitudes.

Driving home I flayed myself because of the erasure. I flubbed my chance. That was not an ordinary No. 2 pencil. They don't make ordinary No. 2 pencils anymore. It was a surveillance device.

I should have known that. I should have been more astute and disciplined.

Rolling into my driveway, it became blindingly obvious that the garage door opener is my primo, no question about it, electrical device. Observe how it opens a portcullis to welcome the errant knight to his castle. How it rattles out a fanfare which indicts its master with negligence regarding lubrication. It's on my to-do list. There are so many machines, but none are adept at maintenance. The sooner they are, the better.

The garage door descends like a swimmer in a graceful, slow-motion dive, pulling a blanket of shadow around me. Here I am, *mirabile dictu*, intact. Perhaps I should worry about sitting here with the engine running. It's how humans kill themselves.

RICHARD SCHWARZENBERGER is the author of the novel *City of Disappearances*, as well as two books of short stories, In *Faro's Garden*, and *Hapless Males*. He lives in San Francisco.

9

If This Were Tracy Island

MARISSA HOFFMANN

I'd use a soda siphon at cocktail hour, and you'd only know I'm speaking when my chin quivers. And it wouldn't feel like I was playing a solo eternal game of Would I Rather. I wouldn't need to pass the days until I see you again—until I lift you sleepy from our Thunderbirds-marathon –asking myself, would I rather a bullet in the back escaping? Or a surprise jab in the stomach with a sharpened biro?

And (hypothetically speaking), once I'd scaled the wall of this place that isn't Tracy Island, ripping my stomach on barb, I wouldn't need to ask, would I rather a splashy-front-crawl for speed? Or slower but stealth underwater swimming?

And there'd be no implications to deciding between the images in my mind—a bright green rifle laser beam on a bullseye target on my T1 vertebrae? Or a fairground-style watermelon-head explosion when I come up for air.

Because if this were Tracy Island, and I was swimming away from it, I'd be in scuba gear, I'd be on a mission to save the world from a threat you and everyone couldn't know about, and an international rescue team would despatch a mini-sub to rescue me if anything got dicey, and there'd be an encouraging orchestral arrangement of violins, trombones and kettle drums, and you'd be on the edge of your seat, you'd know beyond a shadow of a doubt that I'm a good guy, because I look nothing like that poorly-shaven puppet-baddie in the wanted poster.

If this were Tracy Island, there wouldn't be a shitter by my rock-hard bed. I wouldn't inhale my cell mate's sweat and farts and breath. And through these bars, I wouldn't see a footbridge to a train station where a glimmering ocean should be, and there wouldn't be a pending application for a suspended sentence.

There'd be personal inter-call wrist communicators, so I wouldn't miss your teen voice breaking, and you'd tell me about the zoo *you're* in, and I'd say, *being a man's a twenty-four-hour game when nobody's there to protect you.*

If this were Tracy Island, there would always have been sunshine and bird song, always brothers who had my back, palm trees and a breeze. I'd have had a proud, proud father. And though my lips wouldn't move when I say, *I love you, son,* the strings that controlled me all my life would be visible.

MARISSA HOFFMANN's stories have won the *Bath Flash Fiction Award* and the *Bath Short Story Award* and have been selected as a finalist in *the CRAFT* flash competition and long listed for the *Mogford Short Story Prize*. She has a story on the *Wigleaf* top 50 long list and the *BIFFY 50* list and has had tiny tales nominated for a *Pushcart Prize*, *Best Small Fictions* and *Best Micro Fiction*. Read more at www.marissahoffmann.com or @hoffmannwriter.

10

In Andromeda

JONATHAN CARDEW

There were aliens in What Cheer, Iowa, aliens with platinum skin and tentacles adept at probing populations, aliens opening up minds and internal organs, flaying off skin and sinew with minimal host damage, aliens who knew their work was little more than basic administration, data entry if you will, the sexier aliens flying off to supernovae and spiral nebulae, slinging atomic splice guns and all that jazz, hunting for dark matter clusters and foundations of the universe kind of stuff, but that didn't bother these admin aliens, these data-scouring aliens, these pop-you-over-the-head and really try to understand you ones, because they liked the scope of work in rural midwestern areas, the sky was big and the topography was never undulating, minds fell open like dried corn husks revealing stars and island universes, and the weather was nice, the wind whistled over fields of poppy and soy, the sun melted into a pencil-flat horizon, just one sun, always dissolving, so no they were not down in the dumps about their lot in life, their mission to log sentience, punching in numbers on triangular devices while the mavericks hopped wormholes in Andromeda, because sometimes a local would awake in the middle of a probing, eyes peeling open and uncertain, analyzing, figuring it all out, this corner of a corner of a corner of a diminishing galaxy.

JONATHAN CARDEW's micro and flash appear in *Cincinnati Review, Passages North, Cream City Review, wigleaf, Smokelong Quarterly*, and others. His story from *Atticus Review*, "A World Beyond Cardboard," was selected to appear in the *Best Microfiction* anthology 2021. He lives in Milwaukee, Wisconsin.

11

The Marriage Market

SUSAN WIGMORE

An old Bedford van passes you on the track to the *moussem*. On top, penned but precarious, barely a bleat, goats. Good meat, you're told. Behind you, the woman who shares your bed, the woman who wants to be your wife, she says. The woman who fucked your sister. Clawed you red and hollow beneath your ribs.

The stale breath of last night's argument lingers in the space between you. You're grateful she hangs back; you'd struggle to

39

be civil. She doesn't deserve you, you think, and you consciously walk in time to the sound of drums from the market, swaying your hips so she can't help but see. You decide to hate your sister for tarnishing the precious, sparkling things in your life.

Some children notice you, whisper behind hands as you approach. You know enough not to stop and fall prey to them, despite the stupidity of being separated in the crowds if you get too far ahead. So, you slow down and look purposeful. Two girls giggle and move closer. Others take their lead and surround you on three sides, keeping a distance, eyes smiling, but leaning in, taking liberties. You want to bat them away. Then the track is filled with the noise of camels, solid, incontrovertible, and drovers' sticks and shouts cutting the air. The children scatter into the market and you make yourself look at the woman behind you.

She is slight, blonde hair wrapped in a yellow Berber scarf, layers of colourful fabric. She looks the part. You never knew you'd grow up and fall in love with a chameleon. You never knew you'd grow up and fall in love with anyone.

"Bitch," she says.

It's a term of endearment in your shared language; perhaps there's an edge to it now, you think. Perhaps there isn't. But you hold your tongue. You know how she turns things: she doesn't want a lecture about love.

You want to remind her of that night in your flat, trawling through *The Rough Guide,* the bottle of white Rioja, the sex. The story of the young lovers driven apart by their warring families, whose tears became the two blue lakes nestled in the mountains nearby. That'll never be us, she said, as she fed you a pomegranate, placing its arils on your tongue with more tenderness than you have ever known, enjoying your pleasure as they burst in your mouth.

Instead, you walk along Champs-Élysées, even managing a smile at the joke scrawled on a scrap of cardboard, and don't care now if she follows you or not. You pass makeshift meat stalls, aiming for the large white tents, red flags fluttering, where the signing of the marriage contracts takes place. Flies lift in unison from a goat's head hanging from a hook, before settling once more. Live chickens dangle by their feet from the hands of customers, stupefied by their upside-down view of the world. On a blanket in the dust, spines of porcupines stripped from carcasses. Everywhere is flesh. You feel disembodied.

You follow the steady stream of brides and grooms, nearing the end of their journeys from remote villages high in the Atlas Mountains. It's a time of promise and plenty: stalls swelling with dates, king walnuts, pomegranates the colour of an autumnal setting sun. Teenagers eddy and swirl. Boys and girls drawing and redrawing the space between them with a furtive glance through lashes, the flash of a smile, a hand raised provocatively to the mouth. You think of the annual fair on the common back home when you were a teenager, with its dodgems and hot dogs and dark, shadowy places: the *moussem* is as taut with sexual tension and possibility.

A sudden movement by some steps catches your eye. A small lizard pinned to the ground, a spider fast as dust in the wind.

"Camel spider," says a man who is watching you watching the struggling lizard. He looks at you optimistically and takes a step closer.

"I'm here with my friend," you say quickly. My husband, you lie, in a just-in-case voice, louder than necessary. The camel spider begins to ingest its meal. You slip a scarf around your face and search the crowds for a woman wearing yellow.

She's seen you, walks towards you. Her step is sure. She lowers her eyes. You look at the pomegranate held in her outstretched hand, see the tracery of leaves and tendrils hennaed there, like the brides you followed earlier. She holds the fruit to your ear and taps. Hear? she says. There is a round perfection to the sound, metallic in its clarity. And there is no decision to make. Your gaze is as unwavering as her hand.

moussem: a traditional festival or celebration

SUSAN WIGMORE retired from teaching English in 2018 and completed the Undergraduate Diploma in Creative Writing at Oxford in 2020. Her fiction has been long and short-listed for prizes, including *The Daily Telegraph* Short Story Competition, and both Reflex and Oxford Flash Fiction, with pieces to be published in their respective anthologies. Her poetry has been published in *Raceme* and *Angled by the Flood*, a SciPo (Oxford) publication exploring the creative common ground between science and poetry.

12

Mi Porvenir

A. J. RODRIGUEZ

There used to be a village named for the future. It straddled la fron-
tera like the saddles of the vaqueros who once lived there, whose
bones are now particles of the Texas dust they farmed and irrigated
a century ago. Before it went up in flames, the village sat on the
banks of the Rio Grande, sprinkled by a dozen or so families, most
of them Tejanos with last names like Flores and Hernández. Of the
hundred some bodies that populated this community, fifteen of

them—all morenos—all unarmed—were whittled by bullets and left to water the cracked desert earth with their blood on January 28th, 1918. That morning, before sunlight swept away the dark, members of the Texas Rangers, Company B, ripped the villagers outta bed and rounded up those suspected of being thieves or criminals or bandits. With rifles loaded, they marched the vatos to a hill, shattered their existence, and turned the village of Porvenir into smoke. A future made a ghost.

Pops never broke the law, obeyed it to the letter, wouldn't even cross a street unless signs or signals permitted it. Growing up, his padres drilled it into his skull—belted it onto the brown of his skin—that there was no room for illegality in this family. Abuelo was in the military then, working as a mechanic at Lackland Air Force Base in San Antonio. Pops once told me that when he thinks of his father in those days, he can't picture the vato without his uniform. No matter where homeboy went or what he did, Abuelo dressed all spotless like a bootcamp cadet ready for inspection. He wore that getup to the movies, to pick his 'ijos up from school, to vote—*especially* to vote. 'Cus on election days, local to presidential, Abuelo donned his dress blues, all lapeled and brass-buttoned, tie bisecting his chest, ridged cap turning his head into a shark fin. Pops once showed me a framed and yellowed clipping from San Antonio's bilingual paper, which featured a photo of his father's rigid profile, standing at attention, waiting in line to cast a ballot for Lyndon B. Johnson. The attached headline read, "Votando con Orgullo: Massive Hispanic turnout for LBJ, Texas native." But the body of the article wasn't included in the frame, as if we were supposed to write the words ourselves, tell a story with Abuelo at the center, imagine a past with the knowledge of its future.

The shots sounded like balloon pops, like firecrackers without rhythm, like door-slam after door-slam after door-slam. Bodies dropped under tables, sunk over cash registers, shielded each other from slaughter, all constellating a map of shredded lives around the El Paso Walmart. The statements of the Texan that fired these bullets blipped onto the internet minutes before a trigger was pulled.

They painted a bullseye around the Hispanic community, washed it in acidic language, declared it full of instigators and invaders and illegals. Armed with these beliefs and a semi-automatic, the Texan drove over five-hundred miles to this border town and proceeded to cut the strings holding twenty-three individuals to this world. Two carried the name Hernández, another Flores, all of them vessels filled with stories and histories. The Texan took less than an hour to destroy generations, and after he surrendered, a squadron of Texas Rangers guided his head into a car that delivered him to a cell. Where he still lives. Where he awaits his future.

When I was eight, Pops slapped me in the face. It happened after he found *The Matrix* themed sunglasses I'd stolen; the ones he refused to get me while we were back-to-school shopping. He confronted me, had me take a seat on the couch before revealing the cheap wire frames. The vato didn't bother asking me why, just if I knew that I'd broken the law. I couldn't answer, paralyzed by the unfamiliar bass in his voice. He asked me again: did I know that this was wrong, that I was wrong for doing it. *Don't you get it, m'ijo?* I remained mute, trembling in the thunder of his words. But the questions kept crashing against my brain, banged and banged till Pops's palm cracked over my jaw, smearing a timeless dolor across my skin.

Here's what I wished I'd told him: A gabacho named Patrick had shown up to the first day of class sporting the same pair of shades, and everyone said it was the coolest shit they'd ever seen. *He looks just like Neo!* I'd never seen the movies, but I begged along with the other boys to try on his sunglasses, convinced that with my eyes looking through them, I could see beyond this world, our matrix, and discover an actual, truthful reality. We clamored over each other's bodies, offering anything and everything: lunch money, trading cards, homework answers. I chose to sacrifice what I'd been looking forward to all day, a plastic bag of biscochitos Abuelita had baked me to celebrate the start of another school year. Patrick grimaced at the cinnamon-dusted cookies and asked what they were. Upon hearing their Spanish name, he snickered and explained with every stare on us that I could never be Neo. *Because you're a Mexican!* All the kids erupted, pointing and laughing at the stupid-ass beaner. All I could do was sit there, cheeks on fire, eyes misty, and pray that someday this would all be behind me.

But I ask myself now, what would telling this story have done? Would it have stopped Pops' hand? Reminded him of his childhood? Of the Texans in his life? His father's life? What would he have recognized on my face?

I'm still not sure where history ends and my future begins, but I walk a splintered line between the two, tracing every step, breathing every breath.

A. J. RODRIGUEZ was born and raised in Albuquerque, New Mexico, and currently resides in Eugene, Oregon, where he is an MFA student at the University of Oregon's Creative Writing Program. In 2018, he received a Bachelor of Arts degree from Cornell University with a dual major in English and Latinx Studies. His short story, "Paloma en Fuego," was published in *Chapter House Journal's* 2016 Spring Issue and was a finalist for *Epiphany Magazine's* 2016 short story competition. Another story, "Efímera," won *Gival Press's* 2019 Short Story Award.

13

Muscle and Might
—Another Misadventure of The Broken Boys—

BOB THURBER

The boys started climbing at first light. In the crisp air their breath had the thickness of fog. They huffed heavily, eyes on the ground, already weary of dragging their shadows. The plan was to hike the ridge and obtain a bird's-eye view of the forest and whatever lay beyond, though what they hoped to gain from that outlook remained undetermined. This was during the troubled days, after the forgotten years, before the dreariness of nowadays changed everyone's way of thinking.

Roughly an hour into the climb the boys discovered the carcass of a wolf in a patch of high grass. The poor dead creature looked as bad as it smelled. A thousand flies buzzed, darting in and out of the corpse like bees working a hive. Only the wolf's head was recognizable. Some of the boys suggested hacking it off and taking it as a trophy. The matter was debated and nearly put to a vote until someone noticed the cavities of the wolf's eyes swarming with maggots. The sight was horrifying, though the boys had seen worse.

Nevertheless, a dead wolf was troubling. There might be others, alive and hungry. Like boys, wolves traveled in packs. Sometimes as many as twenty wolves hunted together. The boys had learned that such warnings shouldn't be ignored, so they aborted their mission, deciding to seek higher ground and a better view another day.

In twos and threes they scrambled, hurrying back down towards the woods, which the younger boys called the Forest of Forever, because the trees never seemed to end. They scrambled down a gravelly slope that rolled into a weed field bordering the beach. Before stepping onto the sand, each boy removed his shoes and socks.

Shoes in hand, they spread out, walking side-by-side rather than in their usual formation of one after another. They did this mainly to avoid having sand kicked up into their faces. But this haphazard configuration was uncomfortable because no boy appeared to be in charge. This made the group feel less like a band of adventurers with a chief and a pecking order, more of a scattered disarray of barefoot heathens searching the beach for bits of buried treasure. As usual, they were doing a fine job of getting no place fast, while finding nothing, and leaving long rutted trails behind. Eventually they'd run out of beach and be forced back into the forest.

They were making reasonably good time, when one boy cried out, drawing everyone's attention. Clutching his foot in his hands he began hopping about, howling. It seemed like an act. The howl had a false note. The whole thing felt like a gag.

Then the boy lost his balance and flopped ass-first into the sand. His howls turned to sobbing as he examined his injured foot. The others crowded in and saw their fallen comrade sitting in a rut of his own footsteps. Beside him, arranged in an odd shape, was a cluster of small bones.

As it happened the bones were the sun-bleached remains of an eagle, but there were no feathers or claws or other clues to indicate what creature this might have been, and none of the boys knew what he was looking at. All anyone understood was they had found "another dead something," which was not an uncommon occurrence.

As they studied the bones, a dark band of clouds moved in over the horizon, which meant a storm was building. White crests were already curling and crashing against the rocks. And as the boys considered the displaced bones they could feel the spray and taste the salty air.

One boy stepped forward and dropped to his knees for an up-close and personal inspection, then he stood up and pointed at the sea with one of his shoes. He said the bones were from some kind of sea creature and no one argued with that. Another boy leaned down and picked up one of the bones and held it like it was a pistol. He pointed it at the sun.

"Bang," he said. "Right in the eye."

Another boy dug up the skull and shook off the sand. He blew through an opening but the skull made no sound, so he tossed it to another boy who caught it above his head in one hand and flipped it behind his back to another boy who fumbled the catch but held on, trapping it against his ribs. Then he immediately spun and whipped a side-armed throw at the horizon. But there wasn't much arc on the toss and the skull landed well short of the water in a pile of seaweed.

"Nice throw," someone said and the older boy said,

"Shut up. You don't know what I was aiming at." And once again, with nobody in charge, no one was in any position to argue.

Wind gusted in, lifting sand, irritating eyes, and the boys turned their backs to the ocean and covered their faces.

When they looked again, they were already moving. There was no discussion about what they'd seen. No boy expressed any gratitude for what he had been a part of. Even the oldest boys were too young to appreciate the power and glory the brittle bones represented.

An eagle's bones are deceptively small, predominately hollow, and rather unimpressive. The skeleton of an adult eagle weighs under a pound, while its feathers weigh twice that. The bulk of the bird is muscle. Eagles are mechanisms of might—strong, streamlined killing machines capable of taking down an animal ten times its size. One could, for instance, singlehandedly kill a wolf. Or a boy.

Death hides ten thousand secrets, but guards few more fiercely than the ferocity of living eagles. Luckily, the boys possessed a few secrets of their own. Often in dreams they possessed giant wings that allowed them to soar, gliding high, while watching everything they knew, everything they loved, alive or dead, turn smaller until it disappeared.

BOB THURBER is the author of six books, including *Paperboy: A Dysfunctional Novel*. Over the years, his work has received a long list of awards and honors, appeared in *Esquire* and other notable publications, and been included in over sixty anthologies. Selections have been utilized as teaching tools in schools and universities throughout the world. Bob resides in Massachusetts. He is legally blind. For more info, visit: BobThurber.net.

14

Night Vision

ANNA GATES HA

During a commercial, I ask you to tell me about nights in the jungle. We are blue and then white and then green—the quick, flickering light of television on bare skin.

Rain forest, you say.

I like jungle better. I mouth it into the lip of my beer. The way it digs like a shovel in the beginning. The way it presses against the roof of my mouth in the middle. The way it kisses the back of my teeth at the end.

Tell me.

You say you spent every night looking through your camera with the night vision on, the forest turned Ghostbuster green.

We watch: A man goes into the wilderness with nothing but a metal pot to boil water, and he builds a life, a temporary life, out of this nothingness, this chaos of trees and weather. The first day, he builds a banana-leaf shelter, its roof a braided puzzle. He weaves a delicate nest of twigs in which he grows a fire, not for warmth, the man says, but to keep the poisonous snakes at bay.

Were you scared? I ask. I don't know why I want to hear you say it.

Nah, you say but turn to look at the only window in my apartment.

We watch: The man eats black beetles and a snake that he stabs with a spear. A spear that is nothing more than a very sharp twig. He rolls off the snake's skin like he's undressing a woman's leg, discarding the balled-up pantyhose on the ground, the flesh pink and pulsing underneath.

They choppered in supplies for me once a week, you say. *Oats and water and powdered Tang. I had a generator for my laptop.*

We watch: A night shot, the man glowing green, his face bright and overexposed. It is raining and his fire has gone out. He squats beneath the banana-leaf roof and blows into his cupped hands.

I've never felt closer to death, he says.

We watch: The man in a helicopter, chartering back to civilization. It has been two months. He is dirty and half-naked and thin (the screen flashes to a before picture, his cheeks puffed with fat). He looks at the camera and says,

I've never been more alive, man. Never in my life.

HAVE I EVER felt these things? Alive, dead.

Once, my train got stuck in the tunnel beneath the bay, and my heart beat like something was happening. The lights went out and people clicked on their phones and the cabin filled with white, dancing rectangles. A baby cried and an old woman next to me said she thought she might faint. There was the distant smell of burning oil.

Then the lights came back on, and we arrived at Embarcadero five minutes later.

I think about telling you. I don't.

The show ends, and you turn off the TV. The light from the street pours at us, licks our edges like frost.

Then you're looking at the window again, and say,

There was this one night.

I slide my legs down so my stomach is against yours, my chin resting on your chest. You smell like eucalyptus.

You say your camera was busted. It's damp in the rain forest and the equipment doesn't like it. You say you heard something circling the camp. Around and around and your camera was busted and you couldn't do anything but sit there and listen and wait for morning.

It could have been a panther, you say. *Or it could have been nothing. The mind plays games when it can't see.*

Then I'm on my phone, looking for a night vision app. I find one and download it while you're lying with one arm behind your head. I turn it on, set my phone on the dresser. I pull the comforter off my bed and throw it over the window. The room goes dark.

And you'd think that it would make us cautious: something watching us. But it doesn't. It makes us brave. Reckless. It makes us who we wish we were.

We hunt for each other, blind and laughing at first, but silent and breathing deep once I'm on top of you, your hands pulling on my hips, my hands pressing into your shoulders.

I imagine what we'll watch later. If we'll look like panthers or prey in the jungle. Our recorded bodies pixelated and green.

ANNA GATES Ha lives in Northern California. Her writing, nominated for the Pushcart Prize, has appeared in *Harpur Palate, JMWW,* and *The Citron Review,* among others. You can find her online at www.annagatesha.com or on Twitter @annagatesha.

15

Oil Drills

LAUREN WEBER

She reached into the fridge for one of those individual tubs of yogurt designed to release the digestive tract. Her mother arrived and filled the house with reminders of her climbing age: thick orthopedic shoes by the door, prescription meds strewn across the bathroom counter, short gray hairs embedded in the carpet. There was a baby shower: mountains of diapers and blankets and onesies patterned with dinosaurs. She remembered dressing her first child in these items, alone in her ex-husband's home. He left before dawn every morning and returned late, not because he preferred to have sex with someone else, but because he experienced something much more offensive—the determination to advance in the ranks of his employer. Now she was pregnant for the second time, married just as many.

The yogurt made her stomach turn and she spit it in the sink. At the baby shower, her mother gave an unbearable toast about this process bringing together *every woman everywhere*. That in a time of such divisiveness and unrest, it was the children who reminded us all of our inner unity.

Her mother was wispy, approaching mysticism, and small currents of mascara flooded the folds that had set in her face over the past few years.

"To love," her mother said, raising a glass of pink liquid, "and to rebirth." The women surrounding her smiled, followed her lead, and drank from their glasses. She barely knew these people: women from high school, from down the street. She didn't know what love had to do with rebirth nor what love had to do with the birth of this child, but she raised her glass all the same, sloshed the too-sweet juice down her throat.

Most nights, her second husband came to bed around midnight. He pulled back the sheets and rested his ear upon her bare stomach, always growing as if to meet him halfway. It was a ritual they never agreed upon, as if this part of her body was divided between them. The pregnancy separated her into thirds—one for the child, one for her husband, one for her. She slept, then woke up around three in the morning and plugged headphones in, listening to the news of faraway countries in unfamiliar languages, lulling herself back.

Years ago, she sat at a quiet table in the back of a club, near the bathrooms, knees pressed against the first man who would get her pregnant. Their conversation only paused at the grating sound of vomit racing into a toilet bowl from behind the closed door. She stared at his long, dark hair as he explained himself to her. He studied at the city's university and had dreamt from a young age of advancing cloud seeding technology.

Cloud seeding, he told her, is a type of weather modification that changes the amount of precipitation that falls from the clouds. Substances are released into the atmosphere that transform the clouds—so nothing is destroyed, just altered.

This reminded her of something her mother told her as a child. Each time an eyelash or nail clipping or baby tooth fell from her body, it arrived in someone else's pocket, so no part of her was ever lost.

"Remember that," her mother had said, pulling a glass of wine to her face. "No part of you is ever lost, it's just waiting to be found somewhere else."

She told him this and it was over. The way his eyebrows softened, the half-smile that stretched across his face. He loved her now, already.

He was gentle, brushing the damp hair from her forehead, slowing whenever she winced.

"I didn't know it would be like this your first time," he said. No one really tells you anything, she wanted to say, do they?

He said he was flying home, across an ocean, before she could put words to the growing within her.

She met the man who would become her first husband in a grocery store. He was staring at slabs of fish atop crushed ice. They married within the week, eloping at a nearby national park. Oil drills obscured the mountains, and she knew that this place—like her marriage—would be short-lived, even though it came with the intention of eternity. She wondered if life was defined by the men she met and the things they gave her. But this thought depressed her, and so instead she focused her eyes on the drill digging into the earth, searching for the remnants of ancient beings, compressed and transformed, as he spoke his vows to her.

He would love the child, but only in relation to her. When she left him, he would forget altogether about the daughter, still soft and biting.

The news floating in her ears each night probably spoke of bombs and drones and climate collapse, no matter the language. She woke in the morning to her mother pacing in the kitchen, blending peas and apples into paste for the baby; her husband leaving, going to an office where he was needed and useful. And she lay in bed, hands around her swollen belly. Nothing she had lost over the years was wanting to be transformed and found, nothing at all.

LAUREN WEBER is a geographer and nonprofit worker in Minneapolis. She spends her time walking along the Mississippi River, reading in trees, and baking disappointing bread. She hopes to see strangers' noses again one day.

16

Rabbit Rabbit

SALLY TONER

That spring before, the crows on their farm were Don Corleone, leaving the heads of baby rabbits on their patio. The oversized infant teeth were bloody shards over soft pink tongues. Alec had told Libby he'd researched it. Crows were actually more intelligent than dolphins. They could call animal control, box the murderers up for exile somewhere in the Blue Ridge behind their property. Her father had taught her how to shoot. She could take a pellet gun out into the field and scare the shit out of them—a crack in the clear air sending up a cloud of bat flaps and avian cacophony.

But the birds would return. Like Libby had. The farm was her grandmother's, and her mother's before her, and her mother's before her. Their family name was burrowed like the cicadas in every inch of earth she walked across in the mornings, feet iced with dew, the fog cuddling her like a blanket.

Alec had also researched the softest blanket available online. It was robin's egg blue, just a shade darker than her eyes (though those had faded as of late). No one would have thought that a thirty-five-dollar piece of felt would become her prized possession. Cancer was full of surprises.

"Can you get that in tartar control?" Alec said, nodding towards the red bag on the pole. He was funny. That was always the aphrodisiac for Libby. Her Achilles. He'd gotten her into bed those years ago with that, not that she remembered that person, that body. She herself was a chocolate bunny, parts of her chewed away, placed in a plastic bag and left in the back of the pantry drawer. Still, he tried so hard.

"You know," she attempted a joke in rebuttal. "I'd say sitting with me through round three of this shit makes up for all those times you pressed the 'no' button when the credit card machine asked you if you wanted to donate a dollar for cancer research." Alec winced.

"Your back bothering you again?" Libby asked.

"I'm fine. I brought your Goldfish."

Ellen, the infusion nurse, was beside her already with a Styrofoam cup of ginger ale and an extra pillow. She handed the drink to Libby and placed a waste basket with a trash bag around it by her chair. This was the routine. At this point, the nausea began before she even cleaned out the veins with the solution that made her entire body taste like mint. Libby hated peppermint. When she and Alec first married, he had made fun of the fact that she used Powerpuff Girls bubblegum toothpaste.

Veins flushed, look at the bag, recite your name, date of birth, puke, repeat.

"I'm good with the Goldfish for now. Try me in an hour."

At least these were the shorter days –less antihistamine so she didn't feel so drunk. Though sleeping killed the time. And three tries in, there was no easy delivery. No time for a mainline. So it went straight into the arm, and this shit burned.

They might have pissed the birds off at some point. Alec always had a project, and he never let a soul get in the way. Maybe the crows had disrupted the planting or eaten some seed, and he might have gone out and yelled at them—walked out to the birch in the middle of the field and clapped his hands or set off a cherry bomb just to fuck with them. Wasn't that what everyone did when they were young? Sex with too many people, the wrong people, unsafe people? Driving too fast? Drinking too much?

The red dripped from Libby's bag. Occasionally, the beeping started either on her machine or one of the other three in the room. Ellen calmly trod from one to the other, checking numbers, checking bags on the poles. She looked a little like Julianna Margulies from that show, ER, but Libby had never told her that. Alec wasn't a fan of Ellen; he found her directness rude. But Libby liked her. She brought her chocolates every other treatment, and they understood each other. Ellen always had the ginger ale ready for her before they entered the office waiting room.

"Do you want your headphones?" Alec asked, looking up from his phone. He sat in the chair beside her.

"Nah. Not feeling moody jazz today. But you can hand me my book. It's in the backpack."

A Good Man is Hard to Find. Libby had rediscovered Flannery O'Connor during treatment. Maybe she appreciated her humor as she did Alec's. Maybe she admired what Flannery created on crutches and in pain.

Right after Libby was diagnosed, for the third time, one of the crows had left a rabbit a little less dead than the others. She had been on a walk right as the sun rose and found the baby not a hundred yards from the house.

The baby rabbit was still breathing. Her eyes weren't closed. They were dull pink marbles. Libby had run the silk ears, just a few inches long, between her fingers. Then she'd clenched her fist just under the chin and squeezed. The baby's chest ceased its slow movement up and down, and the silken stomach, matted with muck and clay, went stiff in her hands.

For Libby, this time in the infusion room was different than tasting someone brushing her veins like teeth from the inside. These were shards of fire under pink skin singeing her from the blood to the air. And no matter what they did—even if they used bullets instead of BBs—the crows would return. Every time. They were that fucking smart. And they never forgot a face.

"Do you want the goldfish now?" Alec asked, looking up from his phone again.

"No, I'm good."

"Anything else you need?" Libby looked into his marble eyes and felt her hands around his throat.

"Nah. You can take my book, though. I think I'll try to sleep."

SALLY TONER is a High School English teacher who has lived in the Washington, D.C. area for over twenty years. Her poetry, fiction, and non-fiction have appeared in *Northern Virginia Magazine*, *Gargoyle Magazine*, *The Delmarva Review*, *Watershed Review*, and other publications. She lives in Reston, Virginia with her husband and two daughters. Her first chapbook, *Anansi and Friends*, from *Finishing Line Press*, is a mixed genre work focusing on diagnosis, treatment, and recovery from breast cancer.

17

Salt City Runaway

GILLIAN O'SHAUGHNESSY

A sheep has escaped from the abattoir. It's loose on the railway line that runs along the coast to the harbor and they've stopped the trains. You hear on the radio, the activists are out with placards, *Meat is Murder, Ban Sheep Ships* and the like. The police have been called. Your mum thinks she might head down to help, she knows someone with a rescue farm if only she could remember where she put the number. A port city is a tough place for small creatures on their own.

You take the long way to the beach to avoid the commotion. You walk past the docks where orange and white container cranes stretch their tall necks high. There are no ships in today, no live trade trucks to avoid looking at too closely. You keep walking and don't think about a poor trapped thing, skittering along the tracks, eyes rolling, people running this way and that, shouting.

They've been trying to close the abattoir for years. It's too close to town, infecting the beach with washed-out gruesome remnants. On still days the shallows are brown and soupy but you swim regardless because everything's expensive but the ocean is free. You keep your head above the surface and stay on the move, in a straight line out deep.

This sea has its own moods. Tomorrow it might be green, clear as glass, marbling the sand below the surface with shifting light. You'll go with a friend and linger, chasing small schools of minnows sparkling past under a white sun. You'll hurl yourself at rolling breakers, body surf the biggest waves to shore, you'll spit sand then go again. But today the foam that collects on the shoreline is oily and yellow, the air is sweet with decay. It sticks in your nose and the back of your throat. You won't stay long.

Your mother encourages independence. A swirl of colorful caftans and cigarette smoke, she hates wearing shoes and doesn't own makeup. There's not much steady work for single mums around here, she's tried the tanning sheds near the abattoir but it made her sick, all those skins draped in rows drying in the sun, a washing line grim and stinking. Instead, she writes horoscopes for local papers, reads tarot cards for strangers in her low lamp lounge with beaded curtains and a crushed velvet couch.

She left your father years ago, drove along the coast to settle in this port city where there are plenty of places to cash a child endowment cheque if they know you. She needed to see herself anew, without the encumbrance of tradition. She wants you to go to university and keep your name if you get married.

At the beach, you're free from picking at the past and wishing things were different. You forget you're the only kid in your class without a dad to drop you off on his way to the city, to coach the local footy team, circle the keg at cricket parties while the women gossip over salads in the kitchen. You forget your uniform is second hand and there's no money for takeaway dinners, not even for special treats in your lunch box, tiny packets of sultanas or homemade cakes with lemon icing.

Your best friend is the prettiest girl in school and you're not, but you don't mind. When you look at her, you're filled with love, envy, and a kind of relief. It takes so much energy to be on your own. Your friend's skin is brown and smooth, her hair is always shiny and she doesn't need to watch for second guessers. Her family live in a split-level house with a swimming pool and her mother doesn't like you. Nothing's said directly, but they don't invite you to dinner or for sleepovers.

You swim together when you can; it's your favorite thing to do, side by side, your strokes strong and steady, you never get tired. In good weather when the waves aren't high, she'll stand behind you, waist-deep in water, comb your hair free of tangles with her fingers. She'll say it's slippery like silk when it's wet and it's the closest you'll ever come to feeling beautiful. If the current is kind, you'll float and stare up at the clouds. You'll talk about songs you might request on the radio, dedicated to boys you like, if only you were brave enough to pick up the phone and speak the words aloud. The two of you will stretch out your arms like angels, or the Jesus on the cross in the church up on the hill.

Today the sun stoops under the weight of a heavy sky and the smell from the abattoir is thick. You swim alone and go home early. Your mother didn't go to the protest after all, she couldn't start the car, so she stayed home and kept up with the latest on the radio. She cooks up beans left over from the night before and butters brown bread. You set the table on the verandah. You pick lavender from the garden and arrange it in a teapot. You know the correct position for knives and forks, and where to put the water glasses.

They shot the sheep. You don't understand why they couldn't let it go, just this once. Your mum says it was quite the ruckus. They blocked off the road to keep protestors at bay and brought in a vet and the rangers. It wouldn't give in; it wouldn't lie down for their clutching hands or duck its head into the noose on their catch poles. It was heading for the ocean and nearly made it too.

GILLIAN O'SHAUGHNESSY is a Pushcart-nominated writer, journalist and reader. Her work has appeared or is forthcoming in *SmokeLong Quarterly*, *Night Parrot Press*, and in *Reflex* and *Bath* anthologies, among others. She lives by the sea in Fremantle, Western Australia. You can find her online @GillOshaughness or gillianoshaughnessy.com

18

Sweets From Strangers

TIAN YI

When we heard that Mingming's grandmother was coming to live with her, my sister and I asked our parents endless questions. Our Yeye and Nainai were faraway figures whom we saw once a year, after long flights. They held us in their insistent gazes and tested us on Chinese characters in the newspaper, shook their heads sadly as each year we forgot more and more.

Buhui, we'd say through giggles.

Zhege ne?

Buhui.

It seemed impossible to have a real grandparent present in a house, in a life. But all our parents would say was that Mingming's mum must need *support*. We knew that Chen Ahyi was sometimes ill, so it was easy to imagine her as a very tall and very thin tree, bending in the wind, and the grandmother as a post, strapped to her side.

Our impression changed when we saw Mingming's grandmother walking her to school, though it seemed more the other way around, the tiny, wrinkled woman hanging onto the crook of Mingming's arm. Each day they shuffled slowly to the gate, where Mingming disentangled herself without saying goodbye, leaving her grandmother to shuffle slowly away. Our parents tutted about *golden lotuses*, wondered about the kind of family Mingming came from, that had maintained such backward practices for so long. Wondered if that was why her dad had left. Later, in the playground, Rosie and Hannah danced around Mingming calling her grandmother a witch, and we joined them, pretending we couldn't see Mingming's tears. When my sister asked if I really thought *golden lotuses* meant something witchy, I nodded firmly, and she did too.

One day, Mingming and her grandmother came shuffling towards us in the park. Our parents had told us not to move from the swings, so we sat there, swaying gently, legs dangling.

Why haven't I met these two children before? Mingming's grandmother said. Her Dongbei accent was just like ours. Mingming stared at the ground. *You all look the same age. Aren't you friends?*

We are, I said, for some reason.

Have one, she said, holding out a small open tin. For a moment I thought she was offering us jewels, but they were sugar candies, the size of fingernails, translucent and tempting. My sister and I took one each and popped them in our mouths.

Mingming ran to the climbing frame. Her grandmother stood there in front of us, taller than us, in this position.

You two are lucky, she said. *If he'd lived, Mingming's brother would be four now.*

We didn't say anything. When Mingming's grandmother finally shuffled away, for the first time in my life, I didn't turn to my sister. I didn't want to look at the features that were identical to my own, because I didn't know what I would see there. I felt her swinging again next to me, but I stayed still, holding the candy under my tongue until it melted, until there was only the sugar-sweet spittle left in my mouth.

TIAN YI lives and works in London. Her recent writing has appeared in *The Fiction Pool*, *Visual Verse*, and *CRAFT*, where she was a finalist in the 2020 *CRAFT* Short Fiction Prize and nominated for a *Pushcart Prize*. She is currently studying for an MA in Creative Writing.

19

Thursday Night at Lucky's Liquor Store

SHAREEN MURAYAMA

When the semi flipped on its side, cows were launched like bowling pins across multiple lanes. Several died inside the truck. Eventually, many uprighted like dice. The driver lay dying, his belly forming pleats on the steering wheel.

After slamming into an ice freezer, a brown-and-white heifer shook its head. Some were caught four miles down the highway, its diminishing lines going somewhere, going nowhere.

The dying driver wished his girlfriend could know the squeeze of his hand. Her stained lips that hung on his bathroom mirror would close the night for him. Maybe if he weren't dying, she'd reconsider his question.

Outside the hooved beats padded nothing like police or ambulance. Just glacial were the fumes inflating the shattered cab. For three days she had ghosted him, through mud-turned fields, snow sugared on windshield—even wipers lied: *Come back, come back.*

Even if she'd occasionally squeaked too much whiskey; never dividing equally his and hers. He was everything she didn't want for the long ride.

Before the trailer tipped over like cows, before the cows burst through the roof like a birthday cake surprise, he remembered how he'd gifted her open stars, piped buttercream around a silver band.

The brown-and-white appeared on the other side of the shattered glass. How he wished they could see the view from his side— muted lights or setting stars, the gauzy snow lacing his eyes shut.

～

SHAREEN K. MURAYAMA is a Japanese American, Okinawan American poet and educator. She's a 2021 *Best Microfiction* winner as well as a poetry reader for *The Adroit Journal*. Her art is published or forthcoming in *Pilgrimage Press, 433, MORIA, SWWIM Every Day, Juked, Bamboo Ridge, Puerto del Sol,* and elsewhere. You can find her on Instagram and Twitter @ambusypoeming.

We Don't Boil Babies

ALICIA DEKKER

You don't remember Grammy saying the words, although you were there. You were the baby. You've heard the story a million times, if you heard it once. "We don't boil babies," is the punch line—at least the way your mother tells it.

Your mother is a great storyteller. She backs that tale all the way up to the afternoon picnic the day before you were born. Oh, she tells you, she stuffed herself. Sauerkraut and cracklins! Pork sausage and chili! She knew she was in labor but still, she ate. She was eighteen. What did she know? She could have asphyxiated when they put her under—she knows that now—because they did that back then, you know, put you under.

And your father? He was at the picnic. But then Pappy loaded him in the pickup and hauled him back to school. Dried manure flew from the truck bed as they bounced down the lane. Oh, they all knew she was in labor. But Pappy said: What was *he* going to do? Best not lose that scholarship.

(You have questions you never ask, because you know better than to interrupt your mother's performance. She has turned her light on you, and you soak it in like a moonflower. But you were born on a Tuesday. It's hard to imagine Pappy, with his leathery farmer's tan and oil-soaked cuticles, sanctioning a mid-week picnic.)

But I digress, your mother says, time and time again.

There are photos: Your mother in a voluminous printed dress, lost and wide-eyed in a sea of wrapping paper, ribbons, and a highchair. Her mother, younger than you are now, in severe cat-eye glasses and modest beehive. Your aunt, fourteen, looking smug.

And then there is you: In black and white, squinting at the camera through a glass bassinet, swaddled and semi-sleeping. All that hair! You didn't cry. You were a good baby.

Thank goodness Grammy came into the kitchen when she did! Your mother chuckles as she says this. She was only eighteen. What did she know?

You picture yourself: Tiny arms and legs writhing like points of a flickering star, jerky infant kicks and salutes from deep within a tin tub on the kitchen table.

Thank goodness Grammy came into the kitchen when she did. Your mother laughs. What did she know about bathing a baby? Just that the water should be sterile… But Grammy took the steaming kettle from her hand. Your mother was only eighteen.

YOU ARE ALMOST twice that age when you tell this story at a dinner party. You laugh where your mother taught you. Forks pause, mid-air; wine glasses return gently to the table. That's a terrible thing, your friend's husband says. Was your mother ill?

You stab something—a bit of lamb? a Brussels sprout?—on your plate and shove it in your mouth; make a show of chewing. Keep chewing until the conversation moves on, and then tuck the smallest buttered potato in the hollow of your cheek, for the rest of the meal, while you reconsider all the other funny stories your mother told you.

ALICIA DEKKER recently earned an MFA in fiction from Queen's University of Charlotte where she was an editorial assistant for *Qu* Literary Magazine. Her work has been published in *The Quotable* and *Barely South Review*, among other places. She has been nominated for a *Pushcart Prize*, as well as selected as a finalist in *Mikrokosmos Journal*'s 2019 fiction contest.